JN096931

河野優三枝【編訳】

アリエル・オサリバン【英訳】

原爆の歌
河野英子歌集

木犀社

Genbaku no Uta
Poetry after the Atomic Bomb
A Collection of Tanka Poetry by HIDEKO KONO

Edited by Yumie Kono
Translated by Yumie Kono and Ariel O'Sullivan

Mokuseisha

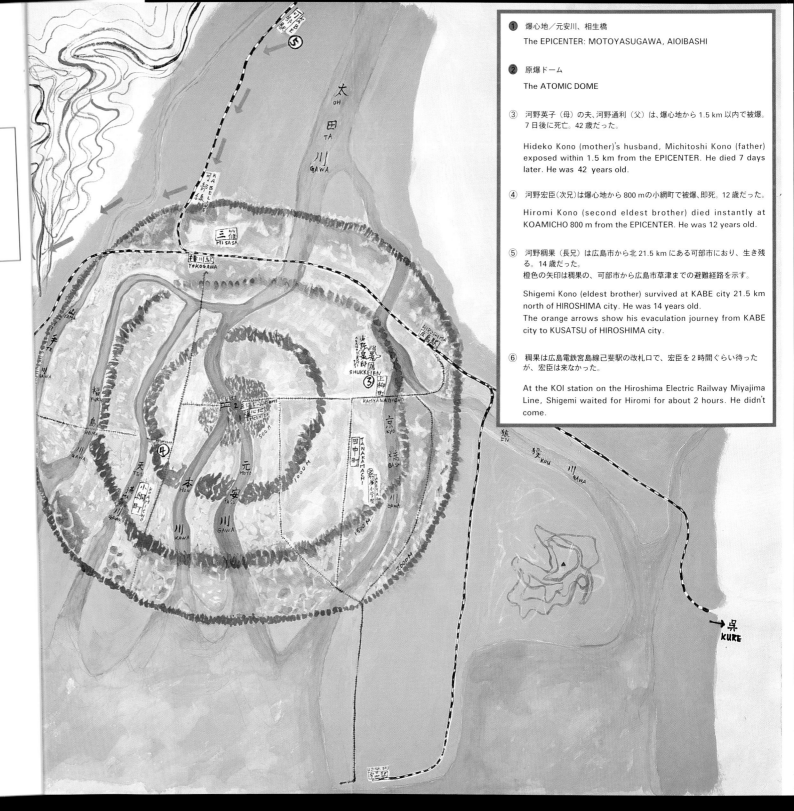

広島被爆地図　1945 年 8 月 6 日午前 8 時 15 分
河野優三枝 作（本文「おわりに」を参照）

ZONE OF ATOMIC BLAST, HIROSHIMA
1945 AUGUST 6, 8:15 AM
by Yumie Kono; See AFTERWORD

① 爆心地／元安川、相生橋
The EPICENTER: MOTOYASUGAWA, AIOIBASHI

② 原爆ドーム
The ATOMIC DOME

③ 河野英子（母）の夫、河野通利（父）は、爆心地から 1.5 km 以内で被爆。7 日後に死亡。42 歳だった。

Hideko Kono (mother)'s husband, Michitoshi Kono (father) exposed within 1.5 km from the EPICENTER. He died 7 days later. He was 42 years old.

④ 河野宏臣（次兄）は爆心地から 800 m の小網町で被爆、即死。12 歳だった。

Hiromi Kono (second eldest brother) died instantly at KOAMICHO 800 m from the EPICENTER. He was 12 years old.

⑤ 河野稠果（長兄）は広島市から北 21.5 km にある可部市におり、生き残る。14 歳だった。
橙色の矢印は稠果の、可部市から広島市草津までの避難経路を示す。

Shigemi Kono (eldest brother) survived at KABE city 21.5 km north of HIROSHIMA city. He was 14 years old.
The orange arrows show his evacuation journey from KABE city to KUSATSU of HIROSHIMA city.

⑥ 稠果は広島電鉄宮島線己斐駅の改札口で、宏臣を 2 時間ぐらい待ったが、宏臣は来なかった。

At the KOI station on the Hiroshima Electric Railway Miyajima Line, Shigemi waited for Hiromi for about 2 hours. He didn't come.

原爆の歌

河野英子歌集

河野優三枝編訳

アリエル・オサリバン英訳

木犀社

Published by Mokuseisha
2-1-20 Asamaonsen, Matsumoto City, 390-0303 Nagano, Japan

First published in Japan 2023

ISBN 978-4-89618-071-8 C0092

Genbaku no Uta

Poetry after the Atomic Bomb

A Collection of Tanka Poetry

by
HIDEKO KONO

Edited by Yumie Kono

Translated by Yumie Kono and Ariel O'Sullivan

Mokuseisha

目 次

　口絵　「広島被爆地図」　河野優三枝作

　カバー作品　「ブロンズのボタン」　河野優三枝作

CONTENTS

    Frontispiece: *Zone of Atomic Blast, Hiroshima* by Yumie Kono

    Cover art: *Bronz buttons* by Yumie Kono

はじめに

河野優三枝

　母、河野英子は毎年 8 月 6 日が近づいてくると、必ず原子爆弾の夢を見ると、私に話していました。本書『原爆の歌』にまとめた母の短歌は日本語で書かれ、もともと母の第一歌集『路』(1967 年刊) の巻末に収録されていた 60 首で、原爆投下後の体験と心理状態が反映されています。私は母が短歌を書いていることはよく知っていましたが、広島を主題にした歌については、母が生きているあいだに、母に問いかけをしたことはありません。母は 1995（平成 7）年、84 歳の誕生日の 3 日前に亡くなりました。

　私の長兄河野稠果が広島で原子爆弾の爆撃に間近に接したのは 1945（昭和 20）年、14 歳のときでした。12 歳の弟宏臣と父通利は爆撃で命を奪われました。稠果は被爆して生き残った、ただひとりの家族でした。家族のあいだでは、原爆のことも、稠果が体験したことも、いっさい話はしませんでした。

　10 年前から私の娘愛子・デイと私は、兄に被爆当時の記憶を辿ってみてくれるように働きかけてきました。稠果は、8 月 6 日に体験したことを詳しく語ってくれました。稠果と愛子のあいだで交わされた手紙が、本書の「おわりに」として、解説の代わりに掲載され

ています。人生の大半にわたって封じ込めてきた痛ましい記憶を呼び起こし、打ち明けてくれたことを、兄稠果に感謝します。

戦争が終わってから母は、厳しい生活を余儀なくされました。母は女学校を卒業してすぐに18歳で父と結ばれ、平穏な結婚生活を送っていました。突然、夫と次男を失い、34歳で4人の子どもを抱えた未亡人となり、大きな痛手を受けました。母は生計を立てるために、島根県松江市で料理店を開きました。その商売が軌道に乗ってから母は、戦時中に広島から疎開したまま預けていた島根県の実家の寺から、子どもたちをひとりずつ手元に引き取りました。私たち家族は再会し、戦争以来初めて家族そろって暮らすことになり、とても幸せでした。母が松江の母衣町に建てた家は、今も家族の拠り所です。母の愛情と才覚なしに今の私たちはありえなかったでしょう。

母は1911（明治44）年に島根県の山奥にある報恩寺に生まれました。文学的環境のなかで育ち、寺の住職である私の叔父は寺で短歌会の例会を開いていました。また、母は女学校にも通い、そこで短歌の手ほどきを受けました。

母は積極的な人でした。知性豊かで洗練された感性を備えていました。聡明で勇敢で、創意に富んでいました。母はすべての子どもが大学教育を受けれられるようにしました。長兄は1953（昭和28）年にフルブライト留学生としてアメリカに渡って学者になり、次兄は放送関係の仕事につきました。娘たちには芸術の道に進むよう励ましてくれました。姉は音楽を選び、私は画家になりました。今でも母の声がよみがえります。

　私は1944（昭和19）年に広島市で生まれました。戦争が激しくなるにつれ、母と父は空襲が身近に迫るのを感じて、母が幼いほうの子どもたちを連れて広島から島根県の実家に疎開していましたので、私は原子爆弾の被爆を免れました。戦争が終わってから私は、子ども時代と中学・高校時代を松江市で過ごしました。1963（昭和38）年から67年まで、東京の女子美術大学で学び、洋画科の学士号（BFA）を取得しました。

　1971（昭和46）年に私は、世界旅行に船出しました。アメリカのサンフランシスコに上陸し、バスでニューヨークへ行きました。イギリスのロンドンに渡ったあと、バスで中近東、インド、ネパールを巡りました。最後にカナダに辿り着き、1973年に移住しました。ブリティッシュ・コロンビア州のビクトリア市で2人の子どもを育て上げ、現在も当地に住んでいます。

　友人で詩人のアリエル・オサリバンさんと私は、母の短歌を、1990（平成2）年から2000年まで、10年以上にわたって、少しずつ英語に翻訳してきました。翻訳にあたっては、できるだけもとの短歌の字義に沿いつつ情感を損なわない形になるよう心掛けました。このような緻密な共同作業をなしとげてくれた彼女の友情に感謝します。

　本書の「序文」は、母の第一歌集『路』への「あとがき」を再録したものですが、母はその冒頭に歌集を編む動機を「私が生きているうちに戦時のあゆみを子供達に書き残したい……」と記しています。今、私はその母の切実な願いと同じように心から、母の短歌を多くの方がたにお読みいただき、ある一家の戦時のあゆみと原爆のことを深く理解していただきたい、と願っています。

はじめに

　湯口磨里子さん、中島洋子さん、澁谷節子さん、丹羽ゆかりさん、音田香織さんには、惜しみなく時間を割いて編集の手助けをしていただき、感謝いたします。

　　　　　2022（令和4）年5月20日　カナダ、ビクトリアにて

FOREWORD

Yumie Kono

My mother used to tell me that when August 6th approached every year, she would dream of the atomic bomb. Her poems, written in the poetic form of Tanka, were originally published in Japanese under the title *Michi*. Sixty of these Tanka poems are collected in this book. They reflected her experience and state of mind in the aftermath of the bombing. Although I was well aware of my mother's poetry writing, I did not ask her about the Tanka poems she created on the subject of Hiroshima while she was alive. She passed away in 1995, three days before her 84th birthday.

My eldest brother Shigemi was 14 years old when he witnessed the atomic bombing of Hiroshima first hand. My brother Hiromi, 12 years old, and my father Michitoshi were killed. Shigemi was the only member of our family who survived the bombing. As a family, we neither spoke of the bombing nor of Shigemi's experience.

Ten years ago, my daughter Iyko Day and I began asking my brother about his memories of the bombing. Shigemi responded with details of his experience on August 6. Shigemi and Iyko's correspondence is included in the Afterword of this collection. I am grateful to my brother Shigemi for opening up and sharing his painful memories, which he had buried for most of his life.

After the war, my mother's life became very hard. She had married my father at eighteen and her married life was peaceful. The sudden loss of her husband and her second son was devastating as a 34 year old widow with four children to care for. She managed to open a restaurant in Matsue, Shimane prefecture. After her restaurant business got on track, she brought her younger children one by one to Matsue to join her after living under relatives' care at a temple. We were very happy to be reunited and to live together as a family for the first time since the war. The house she built in Horo-machi, Matsue remains in our family to this day. We would never have survived without my mother's love and resourcefulness.

My mother was born in 1911 at Hoonji temple, located deep inside the mountains at Shimane Prefecture. She grew up in a literary environment, where my uncle, a priest, regularly gathered with a group of Tanka poets at the temple. She also went to the girls' finishing school, where she wrote Tanka poems.

My mother was a positive character. She was clear in perception and had refined sensibilities. She was intelligent, courageous, and inventive. My mother ensured that all her children had university educations. My eldest brother became a Fulbright student and a scholar in 1953, and my second brother entered into broadcasting. She encouraged her daughters to pursue the arts. My sister chose music and I became a visual artist. I still hear my mother's voice.

I was born in 1944 in Hiroshima. My mother and father anticipated bombing raids and moved her youngest children to a town outside of Hiroshima, which is the reason I evaded the atomic bombing. After the war, I spent my childhood and teenage years in Matsue. From 1963 to 1967, I attended the Women's College of Fine Arts—Joshi Bijutsu Daigaku in Tokyo and received my BFA, majoring in Oil Painting.

In 1971, I embarked on world travel. I sailed to San Francisco and traveled by bus to New York City. After visiting London, I traveled to the Middle East, India and Nepal by bus. I eventually came to Canada and became a landed immigrant in 1973. I raised two children in Victoria, B.C., where I continue to live.

My friend and poet Ariel O'Sullivan and I translated my mother's poems in increments over ten years, from 1990 to 2000. In our approach to the translation, we sought to stay as close to the literal meaning of the original poems as possible. I am grateful for the friendship that grew out of our close collaboration.

As my mother conveys in the Preface to the poems collected in this volume, "I always wished to write down my experience of the war for my children while I was alive." I have inherited my mother's sense of urgency to share her poetry so that readers will gain an understanding of one family's experience of war and the atomic bomb.

I acknowledge Mariko Yuguchi, Yoko Nakajima, Setsuko Shibuya, Yukari Niwa and Kaori Onda for their generous time and editorial assistance.

May 20, 2022   Victoria, Canada

翻訳者のことば

アリエル・オサリバン

　河野優三枝さんが、母河野英子さんの短歌をパフォーマンスしようと思い立ったのは、1989（昭和64）年ごろのことでした。彼女は近くのレストランに地元の画家で友人のウェンディ・スコグさんとパフォーマンス詩人の私を招いて、話し合いの場を設けました。

　彼女はまず、3ヵ月間毎週、同じ時間に、この同じ場所で集まるようにしたいと、提案しました。ただひとつ、お互いに短歌の話はしてはならないという決まりがあり、その訳は、集まる目的がこれから取りかかる仕事の精神的な空間を意識的に作り出すことにあるからだと言いました。

　私はこうしたやり方に大変興味を持ちました。

　私たちは3ヵ月間集まり、そのあとで短歌を読み、パフォーマンスの練習をしました。10首ほどの短歌を取り上げ、ローマ字表記の日本語で覚えました。床に輪になって座り、3人が1人ずつ順番に短歌の一首を声を出して読み、同じ一首を皆で声をそろえて何回も繰り返して読みました。これらの短歌のパフォーマンスはその後何年か、屋外でのイベントや画廊を含め、多くの場所で上演されました。

　1990（平成2）年に入り、優三枝さんと私は、私たちのパフォー

マンスに加えたいと思い、短歌を英語に訳すことにしました。私が日本語をまったく話さないのですから、困難な作業になるのはわかっていました。私は、その困難な作業に、異なる言語で言い換えるよりも、受けた印象を語ることで、立ち向かえるのではないか、それなら、私の「最善」を尽くせるのではないかと考えました。私は、この仕事に全力を傾けようと思いました。優三枝さんと私は、それぞれ数カ月違いで世界の違う地域に生まれたとはいえ、お互いの戦争体験はまったく違ったものでした。

　私は定期的に（週に１回）、期限を設けずに共同作業をするという計画が気に入りました。
　この試みに取りかかるにあたって、自分に課した規則は以下のとおりで、優三枝さんも同意してくれました。

　１．ローマ字表記で５行に分かち書きした短歌の行ごとに、一語一語原文によく当てはまることばを探して、それらを正確に行にあるとおりに書くこと。
　２．思考が思考に従うように、英語を日本語で表現されたものと同じ行に置いておくこと。
　３．英語の行も、短歌の伝統的な形式にのっとって、五・七・五・七・七という一連の音節を保持しなければならない。
　４．私は、どのことばも一字一句問いただして、優三枝さんが示してくれるすべての可能性を書き留めておく。

　共同作業が数カ月を過ぎるころになると、徐々に英語の詩が姿を現してきました。その姿がより鮮明になったように思われる調子を帯びるまで修正を重ねてみても、私にはいっこうにこれでよいのか

悪いのかさっぱり分かりませんでした。私たちは何べんも手直ししては、私が「こっちのほうがぴったりかしら、あっちのほうがぴったりかしら」とたずねるのが常でした。

　こうしたことば探しのあいだに私は、原爆以降の話を綴った翻訳書を、ものごとの意味を理解するために読みました。私は河野英子が、彼女の見たことを意見を述べずに書いている——何の脚色もせずにただ「見たままを、そのまま書く」だけなのだ——ということに気が付きました。知性ある心から生まれたものは実に力強く、おおげさな「観念」などいっさい捨て去って、いっそう詩的です。優三枝さんはいつも、ある種の芸術作品を前にすると、「これは、だめ、観念的すぎる」と、私の耳元で言っていました。

　翻訳を開始してから、10年以上の歳月が経ちました。それからもなお、私たちは訳文の修正を重ねてきました。そのおかげで、優三枝さんとは親しい関係を築くことができました。

　優三枝さんと私は、1986（昭和61）年に、アート・インスタレーションの場で知り合いました。

　私は演劇畑の出身で、詩的な独白からなる一人舞台の台本を書いて、自ら演じるようになるまでは、俳優をしていました。

2021年12月　カナダ、ヴィクトリアにて

TRANSLATOR'S FOREWORD

Ariel O'Sullivan

It was around 1989 when Yumie had the idea to perform her mother, Hideko Kono's poetry. She called a meeting at a nearby restaurant inviting a local painter and friend (Wendy Skog) and myself, a performance poet. She presented her idea which was to meet at the same time in this same place every week for three months. Her only rule being that we were not allowed to speak of the poetry to each other, her reasoning being that by meeting for the purpose, we were intentionally creating a spiritual space from which to work.

I was very excited about this approach.

We met for three months and at the end of this time we met to read and rehearse the poems. We worked on approximately 10 poems and learned them in Japanese. We rehearsed them into a layered chant sitting on the floor in a circle. These poems were performed in many venues in the following years, including outdoor events and art galleries.

Sometime in the year 1990, Yumie and I decided to translate the Tanka into English as we wanted to add this to our performance. We knew it would be a laborious task as I spoke no Japanese. I thought I could approach it as an impression rather than a translation and give it my "best." I felt devoted to the work. Yumie and I had been born within months of each other on different sides of the world, but our experience of the war was much different of course.

I liked the idea of collaborating regularly (once a week) for an indefinite amount of time.

I had some rules for myself in the approach to this endeavour, which I asked Yumie if she would agree to.

I wished to:

1. Explore each line verbatim, writing the words exactly as they appear in the line.

2. Keep the English in the same line as was expressed in Japanese so that thought followed thought.

3. The lines in English must keep the 5, 7, 5, 7, 7 syllabic sequences, in keeping with the traditional form of Tanka.

4. I would query each word and write down all the possibilities that Yumie presented.

After months of collaborating, the poems in English slowly started to appear. They would be constantly adjusted as I got used to a tone that seemed to reveal itself, but I had no idea if it was on or off. We would go over and over the poems and I would ask, "Is it closer to this, or is it closer to that?"

Through this exploration I read translated books of storytelling from the time of the bomb to try to pick up on a sense of things. I recognized that Hideko was saying what she saw, without opinion—just "see and say" without any embroidery. It is very powerful, coming from an intelligent heart, and all the more poetic by leaving behind any grandiose "idea." I always hear Yumie's voice, when looking at certain artworks, saying "No, no, too much idea."

It was the better part of ten years before we had the beginning of a manuscript translated. And we have continued to adjust it over the years. Through this, I found a very close friend in Yumie.

Yumie and I met working on an art installation in 1986.

I have a background in theatre and was an actress before writing and performing my own one-woman shows in poetic monologue.

December, 2021 Victoria, Canada

序 文

河野英子

註　著者の第一歌集『路』（1967年）の「あとがき」を、一部修正、省略して本書の「序文」として掲載しました。

　私が生きているうちに戦時のあゆみを子供達に書き残したいという気持ちは常に心の底に持っていたのですけれど、歌集に編んで上梓しようなど夢にも考えなかった事なので、木村捨録＊先生のお勧めがなかったらいつになっても実現しなかった事と思います。

　過去、先生にもつかず、学生時代から新聞雑誌などに投稿したりして一人よがりの歌は作って居りました。どこの結社にも入っていなかったのですが、15年頃前と思います、木村先生を島根県にお呼びして、山陰短歌大会が開かれた折、先生の講演を聞き私の歌の批評を頂き、その魅力に惹かれて「林間」に入らせて頂きました。

　それ迄作歌は度々中絶し、戦前のものは全部焼失しましたし、作歌意欲も私の急変した生活事情のため失われ、中断の止むなきに至ったのです。

　しかしながら、広島県原爆直後の私達に課せられた運命と申しましょうか、何か神の啓示の様にその時の状態を書き留めておく事を私の使命と思い一息に書き上げたのが、巻末、60首の「原爆の歌」となりました。

序文

　それから幾年その日を思い出したくないので、これら 60 首の短歌は机の奥に仕舞われたままでした。

　歌は女心の悲しみを伝え、時にはよき友となり、恋のよろこびに
戦<small>おのの</small>き、人生の深さを色々に味わわせて呉れました。
　ほんの少しずつながら生活がやや地につく様になって、やっと一人の時間を割き、作歌を考える様になったのですけれど文藻と語学の貧困から極めて　寡作であり、作歌も日記風のものや、とりとめもない文字の羅列に過ぎなくて、全く心恥ずかしい次第であります。
　しかし木村先生の温かい心にふれて始終その懇切なる御指導に支えられ、ここに一冊の歌集が生まれました。本当に有り難く感謝の外はありません。
　自分の歩いた路を振り返りふりかえり、又進むべき一筋の路のために「路」の題名をつけました。
　夫への追慕、子供達の養育、くらしの波間をくぐって時折に燃える女心を、過去さまざまな母の姿を通して現在も尚必死に生き続ける母の像を、子供達の心に刻んでおきたいのであります。

　私は島根県石見の国の片田舎に生まれ、女学校卒業式の翌日に結婚し、広島市に住みました。当時主人、通利<small>みちとし</small>は今の広島大学工学部の教授でありました。
　主人は代用ガソリンの発明に日夜の別ない生活が続き、東京、広島間の往復に度々別居の暮らしが続きました。戦争の最中、主人10 年の苦節は実り発明は完成し技術中佐として陸軍燃料廠<small>ねんりょうしょう</small>に迎えられました。
　其の間主人について歩きましたが、昭和 20（1945）年の原爆により主人は戦死しました。其の時の苦闘は歌に書かせて頂きました。

　幼かった当時の子供達も今はそれぞれの道を歩き出しました。

　私は、今日、松江市でひとり、料理店を経営し、ようやく気まま
の生活にたどり着いたという心境であります。

　　　　　　　　　昭和42（1967）年6月　島根県松江市母衣町

＊——木村捨録［1897 － 1992］。大正・昭和時代の歌人。1919（大正 8）年、
短歌結社覇王樹に入会。橋田東聲に学ぶ。1932（昭和 8）年、「日本短歌」
を発行。その後、1944（昭和 19）年に改造社から「短歌研究」を譲り受
けて発行、1961（昭和 36）年まで継続する。戦後、「覇王樹」の復刊に尽
くし、主宰。1950（昭和 25）年、林間短歌会を結成して、「林間」を創刊、
主宰した。多くの歌集、評論集がある。

PREFACE

Hideko Kono

Note: This Preface is a reprint of the author's afterword of the Japanese Tanka poetry collection *MICHI: The Road* (1967).

I always wished to write down my experience of the war for my children while I was alive, but I never dreamed of publishing a book of my Tanka poetries. If I had not had encouragement from Mr. Suteroku Kimura*, it would not have happened.

Since high school, I wrote Tanka poems alone without the help of a teacher or without belonging to any Tanka group. Occasionally I submitted to the newspapers.

About 15 years ago, Mr. Kimura was invited to the San'in Tanka Convention in Matsue, Shimane Prefecture where I lived. I attended the convention and he offered comments on my Tanka poems. At that time, I was drawn to Mr. Kimura's personality and I joined his Tanka group "RINKAN."

Until then, my ability to compose Tanka poems was often interrupted. All my Tanka poems written before the war had been burned, and I had lost a sense of my creativity because my life circumstances changed so suddenly.

However, I felt that what fate had imposed on us and what happened immediately after the atomic bombing in Hiroshima needed to be recorded. I felt like I had to accept God's will and I wrote down my Tanka poems in one breath. These sixty poems are collected in the final section of this volume, entitled "Genbaku no Uta: Poetry after the atomic bomb."

For many years I did not want to remember that day. Those sixty poems had been stored deep inside my desk.

Tanka poetry can communicate a woman's sorrow or the trembling of the pleasure of love, sometimes becoming your best friend, bringing you to the depths of life.

When my life became more settled, I had more time to create my Tanka poems. However, I was very embarrassed that my writing was poor, worried that my words were meaningless or merely diaristic.

But with Mr. Kimura's warm encouragement, I was able to publish my book. For this I am very grateful.

The title of this book is called *Michi: The Road*. I have turned back often to my past and the road where I came from, and then toward the road where I will choose to go.

Cherishing the memory of my husband, taking care of my children, tending to the chores and activities of everyday life, like swimming between waves, sometimes a woman awakens her desire. I would like to leave deep inside my children's hearts that I was a mother and a woman who has been living in the past and she still continues to live in the present.

I was born in a rural village in Shimane prefecture. I was married the day after my high school graduation. I lived in Hiroshima. At that time my husband Michitoshi was a professor of zymology science of brewing at the National Hiroshima Institute of Technology.

He had been working very hard for the invention of substitute gasoline. During that time, we often had separate lives between Tokyo and Hiroshima. By the middle of war, the invention he had worked on for ten years was finally completed. He became a lieutenant colonel in the Japanese Army, working at the Agency for Military Fuel in Iwakuni.

During that time, I followed and supported him, but the atomic bombing in 1945 killed him. I wrote Tanka poems to express the misery I had suffered and of the experience of devastation immediately after the atomic bomb had dropped.

All my children were very young at that time. They eventually grew up and left home to live their own lives.

Now, I am alone to manage my restaurant business in Matsue and am finally able to enjoy my own time.

June, 1967　Matsue, Shimane, Japan

∗——Mr. Suteroku Kimura was a Tanka Poet who lived from 1897 to 1992. He was an editor and a publisher of "Tanka Kenkyu" and a founder of "RINKAN" in 1950. He contributed to the art of Tanka during and after the war. He also left many collections of Tanka Poetry and reviews.

原爆の歌

Genbaku no Uta
Poetry after the Atomic Bomb

註　短歌は日本語、日本語のローマ字表記、英語訳
の順で掲載しています。

Note: The poetries are written in Japanese, and
in Japanese words using Roman characters, and
in English, in that order.

I

広島の夜の色彩に放つりん青々と人のたましひが燃ゆ

HIROSHIMA NO
YO NO SHIKISAI NI
HANATSU RIN
AO AO TO HITO NO
TAMASHII GA MOYU

of Hiroshima
within its own night's colour
magnesium rays
blue, blue around the people
the souls, they are all burning

焼跡も真夏の雨は降りそそぐ濡れ光れるは誰の骨ぞも

YAKEATO MO
MANATSU NO AME WA
FURI SOSOGU
NURE HIKARERU WA
DARE NO HONE ZOMO

the land is burning
and the middle summer's rain
steadily drizzling
wet and glistening those ones
whose bones are they? I wonder

無気味とも青き炎に光りつつ骨さらばへて蠅につつかる

BUKIMI TOMO
AOKI HONOO NI
HIKARI TSUTSU
HONE SARABAE TE
HAE NI TSUTSU KARU

there is eeriness
inside the blue flame
radiating there
the bones left for a long time
flies are in it eating them

怒りにも疲れし吾等一盛りの骨頂きて帰り来りぬ

IKARI NIMO

TSUKARESHI WARERA

HITOMORI NO

HONE ITADAKI TE

KAERI KITARINU

with anger we are

exhausted and have agreed

to one bowl's amount

of these designated bones

we go back where we came from

ひるも夜もくすぶり燃えつ須叟にして命うばひし何を憎まむ

HIRU MO YO MO
KUSUBURI MOE TSU
SYUYU NI SHITE
INOCHI UBAISHI
NANI O NIKUMAMU

all day and all night
there is smoldering burning
within a short time
life has been taken away
what is it that is to hate

民族の滅び見せたり中空に星が小さきまばたきを見す

MINZOKU NO

HOROBI MISETARI

NAKAZORA NI

HOSHI GA CHISAKI

MABATAKI O MISU

all of our race

obviously is destroyed

in the middle sky

there, a star, small and faintly

blinking, is showing itself

崩れ去るどよめきの中生れねば死なざるものを火の粉飛び飛ぶ

KUZURE SARU

DOYOMEKI NO NAKA

UMARENEBA

SHINAZARU MONO O

HINOKO TOBI TOBU

collapse, subsiding of

many resonate voices

if you are not born

then dying would not happen

fire's sparks flying, flying

血縁を求め疲るる人の群汗にまみれし我もその一人

KETSUEN O
MOTOME TSUKARURU
HITO NO MURE
ASE NI MAMIRE SHI
WARE MO SONO HITORI

blood relatives
exhausted searching for them
the crowds of people
covered with perspiration
I am one of these people

寸秒をおかず次々斃れゆく兵等の顔を被うものなし

SUNBYO O
OKAZU TSUGI TSUGI
TAORE YUKU
HEIRA NO KAO O
OOU MONO NASHI

immediately
no time between, one by one
continue falling
faces of many soldiers
nothing to cover them with

広島に生物絶ゆと言ひつぎて忽ちさわぐ群集心理

HIROSHIMA NI

IKIMONO TAYU TO

II TSUGITE

TACHIMACHI SAWAGU

GUNSHUSHINRI

in Hiroshima

all living things have ended

is being passed on

easily made to panic

it is mass hysteria

よたよたと醜き人の顔ばかり夕べの風に吹かれゆくなり

YOTA YOTA TO
MINIKUKI HITO NO
KAO BAKARI
YŪBE NO KAZE NI
FUKARE YUKU NARI

swaying, swaying
the people with grotesque
faces, all of them
now by the evening breeze
are being blown as they go

一文の銭も持たねばぼろぼろの影ひき乍ら受けし一椀

ICHIMON NO
ZENI MO MOTANEBA
BORO BORO NO
KAGE HIKINAGARA
UKESHI HITOWAN

one cent's worth of
money, don't even have that
ragged, ragged and
dragging a shadow along, I
accept one bowl's measurement

累々と死体重なるその前にむしろ敷きつめ誰も眠りぬ

RUI RUI TO
SHITAI KASANARU
SONO MAE NI
MUSHIRO SHIKITSUME
DARE MO NEMURINU

so many many
dead bodies lying in rows
in front of them are
straw mats laid out side by side
not one person is sleeping

悲しみは言葉とならず只深きねむりを欲りて死者と並びぬ

KANASHIMI WA
KOTOBA TO NARAZU
TADA FUKAKI
NEMURI O HORITE
SHISHA TO NARABINU

for this much sorrow
there is no word to describe
there is just a deep
sleep, that is needed, here on
the ground, alongside the dead

肌寒く目覚めし夜半に聞く死者の怨嗟の声は地をどよもせり

HADA SAMUKU

MEZAMESHI YOWA NI

KIKU SHISHA NO

ENSA NO KOE WA

CHI O DOYOMOSERI

skin is feeling cold

wake in the middle of the

night, hearing the dead's

voices filled with grievances

resonating in the earth

悲しみは越へてきびしき顔となるおのもおのもに骨ひろひつつ

KANASHIMI WA
KOETE KIBISHIKI
KAO TO NARU
ONOMO ONOMO NI
HONE HIROI TSUTSU

the sorrowfulness
the crossing over; a harsh
face it has become
by each individual
the bones are being picked up

又一人死にたるらしき収容所の裏をひっそり車の音す

MATA HITORI

SHINITARU RASHIKI

SHŪYŌJO NO

URA O HISSORI

KURUMA NO OTO SU

again, a person

has appeared to have died

accommodation

in behind this, quietly

there is the sound of a car

頬焼けて娘死にたりみずからを絶ちしあはれも数多ければ

HOO YAKE TE
MUSUME SHINITARI
MIZUKARA O
TACHI SHI AWAREMO
KAZU OOKEREBA

a burn on her cheek
a young girl is dead, by their
own accord, life has
also been ended, poor souls
they are many in number

嫁ぎゆく夢にふくらむ黒髪をじりじりと焼く地獄のさまか

TOTSUGI YUKU

YUME NI FUKURAMU

KUROKAMI O

JIRI JIRI TO YAKU

JIGOKU NO SAMA KA

going to be married

filled up with this dreaming

her black hair is now

'jiri jiri', burning

is this a picture of hell?

Ⅱ

幾千の命吸ひたる川の面に魚透きて見ゆまこと平和に

IKUSEN NO
INOCHI SUITARU
KAWA NO MO NI
UO SUKITE MIYU
MAKOTO HEIWA NI

many thousands of
lives have been sucked away, now
through the clear river's
surface, fish can be seen,
it is truly peaceful

地をゆりて魂泣く声はどよもせりあまねく降れる月光の中

CHI O YURITE
TAMA NAKU KOE WA
DOYOMOSERI
AMANEKU FURERU
GEKKO NO NAKA

the earth is shaking
the souls' crying voices are
reverberating
flooding all over this, the
moonlight, is enveloping

民族の亡び 嘆けるうから等と配給パンをむさぼり食べる

MINZOKU NO
HOROBI NAGEKERU
UKARA RA TO
HAIKYU PAN O
MUSABORI TABERU

all of our race has

been destroyed, lamenting with

this group of people

a rationed portion of bread

is voraciously eaten

次々と人は恐怖の中に死ぬ世界の滅び近づくを見つ

TSUGI TSUGI TO

HITO WA KYOFU NO

NAKA NI SHINU

SEKAI NO HOROBI

CHIKAZUKU O MITSU

one after another

the people terrified

die in this manner

the destruction of the world

draws near; it is apparent

板の上に白く盛りたる骨片は涙枯れたる人が持ち去る

ITA NO UE NI
SHIROKU MORITARU
KOPPEN WA
NAMIDA KARETARU
HITO GA MOCHISARU

on top of a board
is a hilled-up pile of white
pieces of bone
tears have run dry, a person
is being taken away

おびただしく牛馬斃れし川砂を満潮なれば浸しゆくなり

OBITADASHIKU
GYŪBA TAORESHI
KAWASUNA O
MICHISHIO NAREBA
HITASHI YUKUNARI

a multitude of
cows and horses have fallen
in the river sand
as the tide is coming in
they are immersed in water

双乳もあらはに見せて妻狂乱炎天あかき血を流す河

MOROJICHI MO
ARAWANI MISETE
TSUMA KYŌRAN
ENTEN AKAKI
CHI O NAGASU KAWA

both breasts two of them
open and fully exposed
a wife has gone mad
flaming sun, red fire, the
river is flowing with blood

骨壷を抱きて居ればうつせみの夫とわれなり赤き花園

KOTSUTSUBO O
IDAKITE OREBA
UTSUSEMI NO
TSUMA TO WARE NARI
AKAKI HANAZONO

an urn of bones
I am embracing in
this temporal world
my husband and I exist
in a red flower garden

かさこそと夫のつぶやき聞く如く骨壺をわがふりて悲しむ

KASA KOSO TO

TSUMA NO TSUBUYAKI

KIKUGOTOKU

KOTSUTSUBO O WAGA

FURITE KANASHIMU

'kasa koso to'

my husband is whispering

I am listening

to the box of bones that I

am shaking, I am so sad

仮駅に夫の骨持つどの汽車も女子供を取り残し行く

KARIEKI NI
TSUMA NO HONE MOTSU
DONO KISHA MO
ONNA KODOMO O
TORINOKOSHI YUKU

a makeshift station
with the bones of my husband
while each of the trains
leave the women and children
behind as they go bye

身辺の人ことごとく逝かしめて吾が呆然とありし幾日

SHINPEN NO
HITO KOTOGOTOKU
YUKASHIME TE
A GA BŌZEN TO
ARISHI IKUNICHI

those surrounding me
the people, everybody,
have passed away and
I have been out of my mind
now for several days

仮駅の夜露にねむる被爆者に渡さるるものパンと梅干

KARIEKI NO
YOTSUYU NI NEMURU
HIBAKUSHA NI
WATASARURU MONO
PAN TO UMEBOSHI

a makeshift station's
night dew, having slept in this,
radiation victims
are being handed out some
bread and some pickled plums

死者の匂ひ風に乗り来て幾万の霊飛び迷ふひろしまの上

SHISHA NO NIOI

KAZE NI NORIKITE

IKUMAN NO

TAMA TOBI MAYOU

HIROSHIMA NO UE

the smell of the dead

is carried on the wind

there are millions of

bemused spirits hovering

high above Hiroshima

悪臭を放つ死鳥の眼のくぼみ蛆這ひ上がりあがりては落つ

AKUSHŪ O
HANATSU SHICHŌ NO
ME NO KUBOMI
UJI HAIAGARI
AGARITEWA OTSU

a putrid odor
coming from a dead bird, it's
eye cavity has
maggots crawling up, crawling
up, then they drop

行けど尚ゆけど続ける焦土にて鉄筋のみがよろぼひて立つ

YUKEDO NAO
YUKEDO TSUZUKERU
SHŌDO NITE
TEKKIN NOMI GA
YOROBOITE TATSU

going on and on
still going, continuing
in the scorching earth
only steel buildings have been
left, they are barely standing

くるしみの表情持たず死にたりし兵等よ日本勝つと思ひて

KURUSHIMI NO
HYŌJŌ MOTAZU
SHINITARISHI
HEIRA YO NIHON
KATSU TO OMOITE

there is an anxious
expression you did not have
you have passed away
all you soldiers and Japan
has won you are thinking

雨も陽も焦土うるほす糧ならず人焼く匂ひ天地に満つ

AME MO HI MO

SHŌDO URUOSU

KATE NARAZU

HITO YAKU NIOI

AMETSUCHI NI MITSU

both the sun and rain,

the scorched earth's nourishment,

grow no provisions

a smell of burnt human flesh

filling the earth and the sky

相寄りて生き残りたる悲しみを語り合ふ時救急車来る

AIYORI TE
IKI NOKORITARU
KANASHIMI O
KATARIAU TOKI
KYŪKYŪSHA KURU

huddled together
the living, the survivors
are sorrowfully
conversing, when suddenly
an ambulance approaches

梅干しを一つ入れたる握り飯押しいただきつ涙流れぬ

UMEBOSHI O
HITOTSU IRETARU
NIGIRIMESHI
OSHI ITADAKITSU
NAMIDA NAGARENU

umeboshi (a pickled plum)
is put in the center of
a ball of rice
now preciously eating this
tears are no longer running

失へるものばかりにて幾日経む焼けちぢまりしスカートをはき

USHINAERU

MONOBAKARI NITE

IKUHI HEN

YAKECHIJIMARISHI

SUKĀTO O HAKI

only the loss of

things, there has been nothing else

in the passing days

the burning has shortened

the skirt that I am wearing

朝ぎりに手足冷え来し子を抱く死も易々と許されずして

ASAGIRI NI
TEASHI HIEKISHI
KO O IDAKU
SHI MO YASU YASU TO
YURUSAREZU SHITE

in early morning
hands and legs becoming chilled
holding my child close
even death, easily
is not permitted to do

悲しみに実りし吾子を脊に負ひて受刑の如く歩み初めぬ

KANASHIMI NI

MINORISHI AKO O

SE NI OITE

JUKEI NO GOTOKU

AYUMI HAJIMENU

with my sorrow

and with my growing child

carried on my back

like a punished criminal

I embark on a first walk

Ⅲ

人心の定まらぬ夜に娘持つ父達銃をかまへて眠る

JINSHIN NO

SADAMARANU YO NI

MUSUME MOTSU

CHICHITACHI JŪ O

KAMAETE NEMURU

the general mind

is unsettled, in the night,

fathers with daughters

hold onto firearms and

position themselves in sleep

明日こそは敵の侵入あるべしと若者たちの夜毎さわげる

ASU KOSO WA

TEKI NO SHINNYŪ

ARUBESHI TO

WAKAMONO TACHI NO

YOGOTO SAWAGERU

tomorrow for sure

the enemy will invade

this is the belief

many young people gather

every night there's a clamour

夜ひそと貼られしビラか駅の前に平和と交戦の文字だけ赤し

YORU HISO TO
HARARESHI BIRA KA
EKI NO MAE NI
HEIWA TO KŌSEN NO
MOJI DAKE AKASHI

at night, secretly,
flyers have been plastered in
front of a station
Peace and War are the only
words that are written in red

一葉の写真に飾る黒リボン夫よ子の手を引きてゆきませ

ICHIYŌ NO
SHASHIN NI KAZARU
KURO RIBON
TSUMA YO KO NO TE O
HIKITE YUKIMASE

a solitary
photograph decorated
with a black ribbon
husband, hold the child's hand
please take it along with you

なにによる命か明日を生きつぐは「何とかなるさ」皆自暴自棄

NANI NI YORU
INOCHI KA ASU O
IKITSUGU WA
'NANTOKA NARUSA'
MINA JIBŌJIKI

what reason is there
to live until tomorrow,
to continue on
maybe something will happen
everyone has given up

短刀に妖しき光ふくませて子等の額に当てしこともあり

TANTŌ NI

AYASHIKI HIKARI

FUKUMASETE

KORA NO HITAI NI

ATE SHI KOTO MO ARI

within a small knife

an inexplicable light

is being harboured

and on the children's foreheads

put on; these things have happened

防火訓練必至になせし愚かさよ焼けただれたる広島に立ち

BŌKAKUNREN

HISSHI NI NASESHI

OROKASA YO

YAKETADARETARU

HIROSHIMA NI TACHI

fire prevention
had worked very hard on this
oh, such foolery
everything completely burned
standing in Hiroshima

櫛一つ形見の如く持ち 歩く女終りてきびしき門出

KUSHI HITOTSU

KATAMI NO GOTOKU

MOCHIARUKU

ONNA OWARI TE

KIBISHIKI KADODE

I have but one comb

It is now a memento

I carry around

my womanhood is over

to start again will be hard

ひたむきに生きる外なしそそけ立つ髪を水もて濡らし出で行く

HITAMUKI NI
IKIRU HOKA NASHI
SOSOKEDATSU
KAMI O MIZU MOTE
NURASHI IDE YUKU

prepossessed with life,
there's no choice but to do it
unkempt, standing up
hair, with water is being
wet, in order to go out

着るもののなき身軽さやひらひらと裾を焼きたるスカート一枚

KIRU MONO NO
NAKI MIGARUSA YA
HIRA HIRA TO
SUSO O YAKITARU
SUKĀTO ICHIMAI

clothes to put on are
all but nothing, light bodied
'hira hira' (fluttering sound word)
the edge of the hem has burnt
on the only skirt I own

めぐり来る八月六日一握の灰もて汝を葬りたるのみ

MEGURI KURU

HACHI GATSU MUI KA

ICHIAKU NO

HAI MOTE NARE O

HŌMURI TARU NOMI   to second son HIROMI

coming full circle

the sixth day of the eighth month

with one handful of

ashes, holding these, is all

I had to bury you with

漂へる浮草われも根を持たぬ明日を未来と言ひがたきかも

TADAYOERU

UKIKUSA WAREMO

NE O MOTANU

ASU O MIRAI TO

IIGATAKI KAMO

drifting

I am a floating weed

without any roots

tomorrow is the future

saying this is difficult

餘燼のぼる広島が目に浮び来る骨片さがす吾なりしかな

YOJIN NOBORU
HIROSHIMA GA ME NI
UKABI KURU
KOPPEN SAGASU
WARE NARISHI KANA

smoldering rising
Hiroshima, the mind's eye
an image appears
looking for pieces of bone
I was there doing this

原爆に死 にし姑なり老いまさぬ肢態は尚も水々しくて

GENBAKU NI
SHINI SHI HAHA NARI
OI MASANU
SHITAI WA NAO MO
MIZU MIZU SHIKUTE

by the atomic
bomb, mother-in-law has died
age did not triumph
her body and her limbs still
retain a fresh, youthful dew

血を吐きて死にし姑かも子を生まぬ白き乳房は清らかなりき

CHI O HAKI TE
SHINISHI HAHA KAMO
KO O UMANU
SHIROKI CHIBUSA WA
KIYORAKA NARIKI

vomiting up blood
mother-in-law has died
never giving birth
her breast is white, it is
very pure and innocent

姑と呼ぶつながり持ちて住みし家は無惨に散れり皿茶碗など

HAHA TO YOBU

TSUNAGARI MOCHI TE

SUMISHI IE WA

MUZAN NI CHIRERI

SARA CHAWAN NADO

called mother-in-law

we have a connection

the house we live in

ruthlessly torn asunder

plates, teacups, and more than that

おとろへし腕に抱きてつぶやきの如き童話をくり返す姑

OTOROESHI

UDE NI IDAKI TE

TSUBUYAKI NO

GOTOKI DŌWA O

KURIKAESU HAHA

emaciated

holding her in arms

she is murmuring

sounding like lullabies

my mother-in-law repeats

ちちも姑も夫も子も死ぬ秋風に吹かれてあはれ一期一会は

CHICHI MO HAHA MO
TSUMA MO KOMO SHINU
AKIKAZE NI
FUKARETE AWARE
ICHIGO ICHIE WA

father-in-law, and
mother-in-law also and
husband also and
child also, died, autumn wind
blow pity, one life meeting

朱色に燃え立つ垣根めぐらしておごそかに立つ河野家の墓

AKEIRO NI

MOETATSU KAKINE

MEGURASHI TE

OGOSOKA NI TATSU

KONO KE NO HAKA

a vermillion

colour flaming upward, a

burning hedge surrounds

where in solemnity, stands

the Kono family grave

おわりに

河野稠果
愛子・デイ

註　以下の「おわりに」は、著者河野英子の短歌が詠まれた背景を
より詳しく知るために、著者の孫愛子・デイ（アメリカ在住）と、
著者の長男河野稠果（しげみ）（日本在住）とのあいだで 2013（平成 25）年
に交わされた書簡を、一部省略してまとめたもので、姪愛子・デイ
から発せられた 6 つの質問に、伯父河野稠果が答えています。質問
は、彼の被爆体験について 1999（平成 11）年に日本で交わされた、
ふたりの会話に基づいています。巻頭に掲載した口絵「広島被爆地
図」を参照のこと。

　　──1．私の記憶が正しければ、原爆が落ちたとき、伯父さんは
ジープに乗って広島市から 15 分離れた所にいました。最初の反応
はどうでしたか？　　どんなことが脳裏をよぎりましたか？

　私は 1945（昭和 20）年 8 月 6 日の朝、原爆が広島に投下された
とき、広島市から北 21.5 キロメートルに位置する町、可部（かべ）にいま
した。私は当時 14 歳で中学 3 年生でした。私達は学徒勤労動員で、
広島三菱重工業株式会社が山の丘に機械を運び込むためのトンネル
を掘る作業をしていました。8 月 6 日の朝、私は自宅を 7 時ごろ出
て、約 1 キロメートルを 10 分で歩き国鉄横川駅に着き、そこから
国鉄可部線の電車に乗って 40 分くらいで可部駅に到着しました。

可部駅から現場まで徒歩 10 分くらいで着きました。

　8 時過ぎにはトンネルの前の広場に集合していました。そのとき 8 時 15 分に、今まで経験したことのない、凄まじい白い閃光が南の広島の方向から襲ってきて、皆我知らず瞬間的に叩きつけられるように地に伏せました。何かたいへんなことが起こったと思いましたが、そのときは全く新しい型の爆弾、原子爆弾が広島を爆破したとは知りませんでした。

　9 時ごろ指導者不在で、生徒達は可部から広島へ行く街道を三々五々歩き始めました。途中広島市にやや近い所で、怪我をして、やけどを負い、身に着けているものはぼろぼろに破れて焦げついている人達の群に出会いました。さらに広島市内に入ろうと近づいてゆくと、市全体が燃えていてとても入れませんので爆心地から 2 キロメートル北にあった三篠（みささ）の家に帰ろうとしたのを諦めました。一緒に歩いていた広島市の郊外、五日市町に住む 2 人の同級生と共に、迂回して広島市（当時）の南西寄りの経路を辿って丘を越え、山の裾野を通り、五日市町方面に行こうということになりました。その途中、広島市から数キロメートル西に草津があり、そこに当時いっしょに住んでいた私の祖母友代の妹、安代さんの家がありました。

　山岳部の裾野を歩いているときに、パラパラ降る「黒い雨」に遭いました。シャツが黒く汚れるほどの大量の真っ黒な雨ではなく、それはすぐ乾きました。その雨には放射性物質が含まれていたことが後でわかりました。私の祖父、河野茂馬（しげま）（私の名前、稱果と混同しないように）の 2 番目の妻、友代さんは既に三篠の家から草津の安代さんの家に避難してきていました。

　可部から己斐（こい）駅まで 23 キロメートル、己斐駅から草津まで 3 キ

ロメートルで合計 26 キロメートルです。それを西に迂回している
のですから、私は可部から草津まで 30 キロメートルを 5 時間半で
歩いたことになります。午前 9 時に可部のトンネル掘削現場を出て、
ほうほうのていで安代さんの家に辿り着いたのは 2 時半ごろではな
かったでしょうか。お腹は非常に減っていたはずですが、あまり感
じませんでした。ただとても疲れていました。

　祖母友代は到着していましたが、弟の宏臣は来ていませんでした。

　1 時間くらい休んだあと、弟を迎えるために、広島電鉄宮島線己
斐駅に向かって線路沿いに歩いて行きました。午後 4 時過ぎには己
斐駅に着き、己斐駅改札口の中で 2 時間くらい待ちましたが宏臣は
現れませんでした。日も傾いてきたので、その日はあきらめて安代
さんの家に戻りました。そこにも宏臣の姿はありませんでした。

　私はそのままその親戚の家に数日滞在し、無駄かも知れないと思
いながら、弟の宏臣を探しに、祖母と一緒に破壊されて燃える街広
島に初めて入りました。はっきり思い出せませんが、多分 8 月 9 日
だったと思います。普通列車が草津から広島市の西の端まで動いて
いました。そこから徒歩で三條の私達の家へ行きました。家は完全
に破壊され、瓦礫の山だけが残っていました。それから祖母と私は
広島市の至る所を探して歩き回りましたが、負傷者を収容する救護
所などは見当たらず、死傷者の情報を管理する事務所もありません
でした。死体はまだあちらこちらに散乱しており、たくさんの燃え
た黒焦げの死体が火葬されず地に横たわっていました。それは本当
に見るも恐ろしく、身の毛もよだつ不気味な光景でした。祖母と私
はすっかり疲れ果てて、それ以上探し歩くことはできませんでした。

　後でわかったことですが、日本政府と軍隊が負傷者のために仮設

病院を広島市の外れの島に設置していました。しかし祖母と私がその情報を知ったのは、その年の8月15日より後になってからでした。

―― 2. 原爆が落とされたとき、伯父さん、弟の宏臣さん、両親は何歳でしたか？ そのとき、伯父さんは、弟とお父さんといっしょに住んでいたのですか？ 伯父さんと弟の宏臣さんとはどのような兄弟でしたか？

弟の宏臣は1932（昭和7）年8月25日生まれの中学1年生で、もうすぐ13歳になりますが満年で12歳でした。彼は8月6日の8時15分ごろ学徒勤労動員で、同級生とともに原爆投下の中心地近くで家屋の解体作業をしていました。宏臣の消息はわからず、彼の遺体も見つけることはできませんでした。宏臣はとても優しい子で、家では犬や山羊に餌をやっていました。

2016（平成28）年7月28日、その年の8月6日広島市原爆死没者慰霊式並びに平和祈念式に間に合うように、私は国立広島原爆死没者追悼平和祈念館に、父と弟の原子爆弾死没者氏名登録申込書を送りました。

書類作成中、宏臣が属した広島市立第一中学校1年生の犠牲者で、すでに登録された人がいるはずだと思いましたので、原爆炸裂時、どこで家屋解体作業に従事していたかを調べてもらいました。その調査によると、一中の1年生は爆心地より西に約800メートルの小網町（こあみちょう）にいたことがわかりました。原爆投下の8時15分のちょっと前にそこに集合し、さてこれから作業に取りかかろうという瞬間だったらしいです。広島市立第一中学校1年3組の名簿には確かに

宏臣の名前がありました。

　一方、別の情報によれば、小網町より爆心地にもっと近い、約500メートルの本川（ほんかわ）の土手に、広島県立第二中学校1年生が集まっていました。これから作業をする瞬間だったそうです。彼らは原爆投下のときに約3分の1が即死し、あとの生徒は数日中に亡くなったということが分かっているらしいです。もしこの情報が正しければ、宏臣のグループもだいたい3分の1が即死し、後は数日生きていたのでしょうか。もしかしたら宏臣は8月6日に死んだのではなくて、それから数日生きていたのかも知れないです。しかしその消息はいまだに分かりません。思い出しても宏臣は可哀想で言葉もありません。

　私がもっと早く原爆死没者氏名登録申込書を出していれば、2002（平成12）年に国立広島原爆死没者追悼平和祈念館が開館したときに、あるいは宏臣がどこで死亡したのかわかっていたかもしれません。しかし母も僕も広島に足を踏み入れるのを避けていました。母は多分、終戦後広島に行ったことはないのではないでしょうか。幾年も経って、当時のことはもう思い出すのも嫌ですという気持になっていました。今でも平和記念館へ行って、当時の凄惨な写真を見たくないです。母も同じ気持ちだったと思います。母も私もあの惨状をこの目で見ているので、当時のあまりにも酷い光景を思い出したくなかったのでした。

　——3．おばあちゃんの短歌には、多くの死、死に様、破壊の証人としての提示があります。原爆投下後、何日目に広島市に入って来られたのですか？　お父さんの臨終には間に合ったのですか？

おわりに

　多分8月9日のことだと思いますが、父通利が勤務していた山口県岩国陸軍燃料廠 捜索隊の一人が市の中心地とその周辺地域を捜索していました。いくつかあった周辺地域の仮治療所の一つで重症の負傷者の中に横たわる通利を発見しました（今、はっきりとはどこの仮治療所だったか覚えていません）。どうして父通利は、8時15分に爆心地近くを歩いていたのでしょうか。それは私達が住んでいた、広島の北にある借家をもうすぐに立ち退かなければならず、父は次に家族が住む家を探さなければならなかったからです。

　1945（昭和20）年3月には、空襲に備えての強制立ち退きのため、長年住んだ田中町42番地から移転し広島電鉄路線井の口の家に4カ月間住みました。さらに6月に広島市の北の端にある三篠2丁目に転居しました。ところが三篠に移ったら、あいにくその一帯も近く強制立ち退きをすることになりました。父通利はまた借家探しをしなくてはならない羽目になったのでした。
　月曜日の朝、8月6日、父は三篠の家を7時に出ました。本来ならば岩国の勤務先に着いているはずでした。しかしその朝は、7時に家を出て、8時15分、家族が住む新しい借家を探しに、爆心地から1.35キロメートル以内にある名所浅野泉邸（現在の縮景園）近くを友人と歩いていたという話でした。
　実に不運と言わざるを得ませんでした。

　8月9日の夜、負傷した父通利を山口県の岩国市にある岩国陸軍病院へ運んで行く途中、草津は岩国へ行く通り道なので、捜索隊員達は親切にも、わざわざ草津の祖母の妹の家の前に車を停め、父を数分間私に引き会わせてくれました。
　翌8月10日、私は父に会いに岩国へ行きました。岩国は山口県

で最も東側に位置し、広島県に隣接しています。広島から汽車で1時間かかりました。父は陸軍病院のベッドに重傷を負って横たわっていました。顔や体は焼け爛れ、危篤状態でした。しかし私が近づくと、父は「稠果」とつぶやきました。多分ようやくの思いで発することができた一言だったでしょう。「はい」と答えただけで私は絶句しました。あきらかに父は何も見えていなかったでしょうが、私がいることを感知したのでした。後で、どんな気分か、何が起こったのか、爆発はどんなぐあいだったかなどと、聞けばよかったと後悔しましたけれども、もちろん父は答えることはできなかったでしょう。

　翌8月11日、私は汽車に乗り、島根県井野村の報恩寺の実家に疎開していた母に会いに行きました。母に広島の惨事を知らせたのは、翌12日でした。草津の親戚の家にも報恩寺にも電話がなかったのでした。翌8月13日朝早く、母は急いで岩国へ出発し、私は報恩寺で数日休みました。母が岩国の病院に着いたとき、父はすでに8月12日に亡くなっていました。

　母と私は父の臨終に間に合いませんでしたが、ともかく私は父が生きているときに会えました。

　ところが8月14日、岩国はアメリカ軍のB29爆撃機によって大きな被害を受けました。(私はいまだにアメリカが、戦争末期になってなぜ爆撃したのか理解できません。8月9日には長崎に第2の原子爆弾を投下し、ソヴィエト連邦が参戦し、中国東北部の満洲に侵入しました。日本軍降伏は目に見えていました)。戦後すぐ、私は岩国陸軍燃料廠を訪ねました。アメリカ軍の標的になった敷地内には直径10メートル近くの大きな穴がいくつもあいていました。そのとき母は燃料

廠の構内にある仮宿舎に滞在しておりましたが、幸運にも難を逃れています。

8月16日から、母と私は一緒に広島の被災地を訪れています。前に話しましたように、私達は宏臣の死体を見つけることも遺灰を受け取ることもできませんでした。そのようなことは、まったくもって不可能でした。

――4．戦後、おばあちゃんは商売に成功し、子供たちを一人前に養育することができました。未亡人となって、悲劇的な出来事を乗り越えて、成功することができたことに何か付け加えることはありますか？　どのように乗り越えたのでしょうか？

英子、つまり私の母、君からすると「おばあちゃん」（「おばちゃん」というと「伯母」という意味がある）はいろいろな分野に長けていて、特に文才もあり、短歌を作っていました。母の1歳下の弟で、報恩寺の跡取りだった宏道も短歌を詠み、秀でた才能で名を知られていました。英子の才能は文学にとどまらず、優れた計画性と実行力を持ち合わせていました。私が特に感心するのは、これは良いと思ったことを、それ相当の下調べをしたうえで、たとえそれが将来、実を結ぶかどうか確証がなくても、まずやってみるという勇気でした。起業家的能力を持っており、それがのちに不動産取引で発揮されることになりました。

私が思うに、その能力は、母が料理屋を開いたときに功を奏しました。ただし君の伯母、眞里子がのちに私に語ったことによれば、母は当時、そのような飲食業を続けていくのが嫌だったらしいで

104

す。だが 1940（昭和 15）年から 50（昭和 25）年初期という時代に、
4 人の子供を育てるために多くの元手を必要とせず利益をあげるに
は、小さな料理店を営むくらいしかないと母には分かっていたので
しょう。

そのうえ、母は非常に魅力的で気さくな人柄だったので、ほぼ例
外なく人に好かれました。他人に嫌な思いをさせず、知的な会話が
でき、特に若いころは容姿も美しかったです。

―― 5．お母さんの生い立ちや、お父さんと出会ったいきさつを
知っていますか？

母英子は、島根県那賀郡（現在は浜田市に合併されました）、井野
村にある曹洞宗の禅寺、報恩寺の椿活宗といわ夫婦の三女として生
まれました。曹洞宗は臨済宗、黄檗宗と並ぶ禅宗の宗派の一つです。
戦前、報恩寺は島根県西部で最も名声のある、参拝客の絶えない寺
の一つでした。当時は檀家も多く、財政的にも潤っていました。檀
家からの寄付も多く、広大な水田を所有し、近隣の農家に貸し付け
たりもしていました。そのため、母は女学校レベルの教育を受ける
ことができたのでした。当時、このような田舎の農村地帯で、母と
同じような教育を受けられる女子はほとんどいませんでした。

父通利と英子は、河野家と椿家のまたいとこの関係に当たります。
椿が英子の旧姓です。おそらく、二人は結婚前、ほとんど会話をす
る機会もなかったと思われます。結婚前のエピソードとして、私の
祖父河野茂馬（通利の父）は当時、遠縁に当たる椿家によい娘（私の母）
がいるというのを知り、1928（昭和 3）年のことでしたでしょう、
英子の母いわとその他椿家の年長者と話をするため（私の記憶が正

しければ、英子の父、活宗はこのときすでに亡くなっていました）椿家を訪れました。部屋で茂馬といわが話をしていますと、英子がお茶を持ってきました。茂馬は一目で英子を気に入り、彼女が部屋を出るなり「なんとよい娘だ」といって感心していたそうです。ここから、二人の結婚話は進みました。1929年、英子18歳、通利27歳は結婚しました。私を産んだとき母はまだ19歳でした。

　　—— 6．お父さんの思い出はありますか？　どんな人でしたか？

　父通利は旧制官立広島高等工業学校教授で醸酵学の研究をしていました。1940（昭和15）年に技術責任者になり、のちに日本軍の中佐として陸軍燃料機関に勤めました。ガソリンのようにオクタン価の高い燃料を農作物から作り出すという大きな研究プロジェクトを担当していました。当時、いま私が住んでいる調布に近い東京、府中にあった燃料機関の本部と岩国センターで一緒だった年下の研究員、福井謙一博士は、戦後、京都大学の化学教授となり、1981（昭和56）年、物理化学理論の発展に一石を投じた功績でノーベル賞を受賞しました。通利自身も、1940年代に高オクタンアルコールの抽出に関する研究で日本軍より技術賞を受賞しています。

　君の母親の名前は優三枝で、「ゆ」は「優秀」、「み」は「三」、「え」は「木の枝」を意味しています。通利が自らの研究で、三つの優れた方向性を発見したときに生まれた子だという逸話があります。いずれにしろ通利は学者であり教師でありました。また、通利の父、つまり私の祖父河野茂馬も学校教師であり、最後は校長となった人です。そして通利も私も、教授となりました。

　通利は非常に論理的で厳格、生真面目な人でした。のちに見つかった日記や手紙からは、父が母をとても愛していたことがわかります。二人の結婚は、両家の親が取りしきった、昔ながらの典型的な見合い結婚でした。

　いつだったかはっきり覚えていませんが、1944（昭和19）年の暮れか1945年初め、広島が空襲を受ける可能性に気づいていた通利は、妻英子と幼いほうの子供たちを英子の実家、島根県井野村の報恩寺に避難させることを決断しました。都市から離れた田舎の農村地域です。そのとき疎開したのは、34歳の英子（1911年生まれ）、8歳の祥三（1937年生まれ）、4歳の眞里子（1941年生まれ）、そしてまだ幼児だった君の母親、優三枝（1944年生まれ）でした。一方、広島に残ったのは42歳の通利（1902年生まれ）、77歳の友代（通利の義母、父茂馬の後妻、1868年生まれ）、14歳の稠果（1930年生まれ）、12歳の宏臣（1932年生まれ）でした。

　父の決断は、的確で思慮深いものだったと思います。広島への爆撃が差し迫っていることは想像できる状況でした。ともかく、英子、祥三、眞里子、優三枝は疎開者として生き残り、広島に残った4人中3人は、直接的、間接的に原子爆弾の爆発によって1950（昭和25）年には皆亡くなりました。稠果だけが死なずに、今もってこうして生き長らえています。

2013（平成25）年3月15日　東京にて

AFTERWORD

Shigemi Kono
Iyko Day

Note: This afterword is a summary of the letters exchanged between Hideko Kono's grandchild Iyko Day (Massachusetts, USA) and her elder son Shigemi Kono (Tokyo, Japan) in 2013 in order to further contextualize her poetry. Shigemi Kono's narrative was produced in respons to his niece Iyko Day's 6 questions, which were based on an earlier conversation they had in 1999 in Japan about his experience surviving the atomic bomb. See frontispiece, *Zone of Atomic Blast, Hiroshima*.

——**Q. 1** If I remember correctly, you were in a jeep only 15 minutes outside of Hiroshima when the bomb dropped. What was your initial reaction? Do you remember what was going through your head?

I was in Kabe, a town about 21.5 kilometers north of Hiroshima City (administrative boundary), when in the morning of August 6th, 1945, the atomic bomb blasted over Hiroshima. I was 14 years old, in the third year of middle school (chugakko) and we (students) were helping dig out tunnels on the mountain hill to accommodate machines for the Mitsubishi Machinery. The morning of August 6th, I left my home in around 7 o'clock. I walked about 1 km in 10 minutes to reach Yokokawa station and I got on the Kabe line to Kabe station, it took 40 minutes. And I walked from Kabe station to the mountain hill in 10 minutes.

At 8 o'clock we gathered in an open field in front of the tunnels. Then, at 8:15 am, there was a tremendous flash of white light coming from the direction of Hiroshima and everybody instinctively and instantly lay down on the ground. We thought that something unusual happened, but we had no way of knowing that it was a completely new type of bomb—an atomic bomb that had blasted over Hiroshima. Around 9 o'clock we students, unsupervised, started walking on foot in a group back to the city. As we came fairly near Hiroshima, we met a number of people who were all wounded and burned wearing only torn and smudged clothes. When we further approached the city, we saw the whole city was burning and I gave up entering the city and getting back to my house in Misasa, which was about 2 kilometers north of the center of the bomb blast. Together, with two of my classmates, walking in the same direction toward Itsukaichimachi, we took a south-westerly route, crossing hills for me to go to Kusatsu. It was several kilometers west of Hiroshima, where there was a house of my step-grandmother's sister Yasuyo.

In the middle of our walking we encountered black rain (known later to contain radioactive stuff), it did not leave a black stain on my shirt, it dried quickly. My step-grandmother, Tomoyo, second wife of my grandfather, Shigema (not to be confuse with my name Shigemi) Kono, was already there having escaped from our Misasa house.

It is 23 km from Kabe to Koi, and from Koi to Kusatsu it is 3 km, the total distance was 26 km. But we walked south-west, so we walked 30 km in 5 and a half hours. I left the worksite in Kabe at 9 am, and arrived exhausted, dragging myself to Yasuyo's house at 2:30 pm. I should have been hungry but I wasn't. I was just tired.

I saw my step-grandmother but not my brother Hiromi.

I rested for an hour then I walked along beside the tracks to Koi station on the Hiroshima/Miyajima line to see if my brother was coming. I arrived at Koi station around 4 pm and I waited for Hiromi inside of the station for about 2 hours. But he didn't come. The sun started to set, so I gave up and went back to Yasuyo's house. Hiromi was not there either.

I stayed there in my relative's house several days and then entered the city for the first time to search for my brother Hiromi in vain. I do not remember precisely the date when I first entered the devastated and burned city, but it was probably August 9th. I went to the city with my step-grandmother. There was a local train running to the western end of the city, and beyond that we went on foot to the site of our house which was completely burned and there remained only debris. After that we spent time looking around some parts of the city, but as far as we walked, we did not find any rescue places to accommodate the wounded and there were no administrative offices to handle information on those dead and wounded. Dead bodies were still scattered around here and there. It was indeed a hideous, horrible, eerie scene as still many burned and charred bodies were lying down on the ground without cremation. We had already lost our strength to go to any other places.

Much later I learned that there was an island of Hiroshima City where the government and the Army set up make-shift hospitals for those wounded. But, in days before August 15th 1945, my step-grandmother and I did not have any means to know such information.

——Q. 2   How old were you, your brother Hiromi, and your parents when the bomb dropped? Were you living with your brother and father at the time?   Can you describe your relationship to your brother?

Hiromi, my younger brother, was almost 13 years old, born August 25th 1932 and a first-year student of middle school. He was working with his classmates at 8:15 am on August 6th, helping to demolish houses pretty close to the blast center. After all, we have never found his body. Hiromi was a very sweet boy. He used to feed dogs and goats.

On July 28, 2016, I wanted to get ready for August 6 Hiroshima Atomic Bomb Victims Memorial Ceremony. I sent the Name Registration Application Form of my father and my brother to Hiroshima National Peace Memorial Hall for the Atomic Bomb Victims.

During the process of making this application, I was wondering if my brother who was a student of Hiroshima City Daiichi Middle School's classmates had been registered as victims already. I asked the office to research where these students were at the house demolition work. The result found that these the first-grade, Hiroshima City Daiichi Middle School students were 800 meters west of the epicenter of the Atomic Bomb at Koamicho. They were gathering together just before 8:15 and at that moment had just start to work, when the atomic bomb was dropped. Surely, I would find a register with my brother Hiromi's name in a first-grade student, class 3, Hiroshima City Daiichi Middle School.

On the other hand, according to a different source of information, the first-grade students of Hiroshima Prefecture Daini Middle School were gathering together at that moment just starting to work at the bank of Honkawa river located 500 meters from the epicenter, so much closer than Koamicho. One third of students were killed instantly and the other students remained alive for few days. If this information was true, if my brother Hiromi did not die on August 6, he may have lived for few days. But this is unknown to the present day. Thinking about him makes me terribly sorrowful and I have no words to express.

If I had registered at an earlier time when Hiroshima National Peace Memorial Hall for the Atomic Bomb Victims had opened in 2002, I could have found out where my brother Hiromi died. But my mother and I avoided entering Hiroshima City. I doubt my mother ever entered Hiroshima after the war. As time has passed, I have made more distance from remembering about Hiroshima. Even now, I avoid visiting Hiroshima Peace Memorial Museum to see the gruesome photographs taken at that time. My mother would have had the same feelings as me. My mother and I have experienced seeing the horrible sight of Hiroshima City by our own eyes, we didn't want to remember this again.

——**Q. 3**   Obaachan's poetry suggests that she was a witness to a lot of death, dying, and destruction. From the time that the bomb dropped, how long did it take her to come to the city? Did she see your father while he was still alive?

I remember that perhaps on August 9th, a staff member of the Iwakuni Army Fuel Center where my father worked, searched around the city and its peripheral areas. He found my father Michitoshi among the severely wounded in one of those make-shift treatment centers (I now do not remember exactly where that center was located). Why was he in an area fairly close to the center of the bomb blast at 8:15? Because our rented house in the north of Hiroshima was soon to be evacuated and my father had to find another house for us to live.

In March 1945, we had to follow the forced eviction order to prepare for an air raid, we moved to the house in Inokuchi near Hiroshima railway line Inokuchi station for 4 months from our long-time residence in 42-banchi Tanaka machi. In June, we moved to 2-choume Misasa located at the most north edge of town in Hiroshima. Unfortunately, after we moved in the house in Misasa, we had to evacuate this area again. My father Michitoshi had to search for a rental house for his family again.

On Monday morning, August 6th, he left the house in Misasa at 7 o'clock. He usually went to Iwakuni, his work place. But that morning, he left at 7 o'clock and he and his friend went to search for a rental house. This was about 8:15 near the famous house Asanoizumitei (Shukukeien), 1.35 km from the epicenter.

It brought him such misfortune.

On the way to take him to the Iwakuni army hospital on the night of August 9th, they kindly made a detour to show him to me in front of the already mentioned house of my step-grandmother's sister.

I went to Iwakuni to see my father the next day probably on August 10. Iwakuni is located in the most eastern side of Yamaguchi Prefecture, adjacent to Hiroshima Prefecture and it took about an hour by train from Hiroshima. At the army hospital, my father lay down on a bed and looked very badly wounded and damaged. His face and body were burned critically. But when I approached him, he muttered "Shigemi." That was the only word he could perhaps muster to pronounce. I said "Yes" and then was speechless. Obviously, he could not see anything, but sensed that it was me. I regretted later that I did not ask him how he felt and how it happened, and what the blast was like. But probably he would not be able to answer those questions anyway.

The next day on August 11th I took a train and arrived in Hoonji at Ino, Shimane Prefecture, my mother Hideko's parental home on August 12th, if my memory is correct, to tell my mother all about the situations. Neither my relatives in Kusatsu nor Hoonji temple had a telephone. And probably early the next day on August 13th, my mother hurried to Iwakuni while I stayed in Hoonji for a few days. When my mother reached the hospital, she found that my father was already dead. He died actually on August 12th.

My mother and I could not be present while my father was finishing his life, but at least I saw him alive.

Then on August 14th, Iwakuni was very badly bombed by US

bombers B29 (I still do not understand why they bombed that city that late—the second atomic bomb had been dropped on Nagasaki on August 9th, Soviet Union joined the war and started invading Manchuria on the 9th, hence the Japanese surrender was to be obvious and imminent). After the end of war, I visited the Army Center for Military Fuel in Iwakuni. Just in front of the Army Fuel Center which was targeted, there were a quite few huge holes of about 10 meters in diameter. It was lucky that Hideko survived the bombing while staying at a make-shift hotel on the premises of the Fuel Center.

On August 16th, my mother and I started to enter the disaster area in Hiroshima City. As already written, we could not find Hiromi's body. We have not obtained his ashes. It was simply impossible.

——Q. 4   After the war Obaachan became a successful business owner and was able to support her children financially. Is there anything you would want to say about how she was able to accomplish what she did, given that she was a widow in the aftermath of such a tragic event? How did she do it?

Yes, Hideko, my mother or Obaachan ("Obachan" could mean "aunt") was a very able person in many fields, gifted with literary talent, such as composing Tanka. Her brother named Hiromichi, heir of Hoonji Temple priesthood, and one year younger than Hideko, was an excellent Tanka poet and fairly well known. Her talents were, however, not limited to a literary field, she was very good at planning and executing her plans. What I admire most is that she had the guts to start something good after some due study, even though the future results were not necessarily very obvious. That was an entrepreneurial ability. Such an ability was later shown in real estate deals.

I think those talents made her quite successful when she opened a restaurant bar. Mariko, our sister and your aunt, however, told me later that Hideko did not like to continue it, or at all to manage such a restaurant business. But she perhaps realized in those days in the 1940s and early 1950s, that the only business she could launch without too much capital to make money to support her four children, was to run a small restaurant.

Besides, she was a very charming and friendly woman and almost all who met her immediately came to like her. She conversed with other people very intelligently without hurting their feelings. Furthermore, she was actually very pretty, particularly when she was young.

——**Q. 5**   Do you have any information about her upbringing, or how she met your father?

My mother Hideko was the third daughter of Kasshu and Iwa Tsubaki of Hoonji, Soto Sect of the Buddhist Temple located in Ino-mura, Naka-gun (now incorporated as part of Hamada City), Shimane Prefecture. Soto Sect is one of the three sects of Zen Buddhism beside Rinzai and Oubaku. Before the war, Hoonji was one of the prestigious and busy temples in the western part of Shimane Prefecture. At that time the temple had a large number of parishioners and was financially well-supported. It received a lot of donations from parishioners and it itself owned large areas of rice paddy fields which were rented out to farmers nearby. Thus, my mother could afford getting a secondary school education which was very rare among the young girls of the same age group living in dominantly rural-agricultural villages at that time.

Michitoshi and Hideko were second cousins in the Kono-Tsubaki family lineage. Tsubaki was her maiden name. Probably, they had not much chance to talk to each other before their wedding. There was an episode that before the marriage Shigema, my grandfather, father of

Michitoshi, knew that there was a nice girl (my mother) in the remotely related Tsubaki family and he went there probably in 1928 to talk to her mother, Iwa and senior members of the Tsubaki family (father, Kasshu was already dead if I knew correctly). Then when Shigema and her mother were talking, Hideko came into the room to serve green tea for them. Shigema was instantly impressed with her and said "Oh, she is very nice" after she had left. Those words made a start towards marriage. When Michitoshi and Hideko got married in 1929 she was 18 years old and he was 27 years old. When I was born, she was only 19 years old.

——**Q. 6** Do you have memories of your father? What was he like?

My father Michitoshi was a professor of zymology (science of brewing) at National Hiroshima Institute of Technology and since 1940 became a technical officer, later with a rank of lieutenant colonel in the Japanese Army, working at the Agency for Military Fuel. He worked on a big study project of how to obtain high octane gasoline-like fuel from agricultural products. It happened that his junior colleague working together at that time at the headquarters of the agency in Fuchu, Tokyo (close to Chofu I am now living) and at Iwakuni Center was Dr. Ken'ichi Fukui, who after the war became professor of chemistry at Kyoto University and in 1981 became a Nobel Prize laureate for a breakthrough in developing physico-chemical theory. Michitoshi himself was awarded a Japanese army technical prize in the 1940s for advancing a needed study in getting high octane alcohol.

Your mother's name is Yumie. "Yu" stands for excellent or splendid, "mi" means three, and "e" indicates tree branch. There was an anecdote that Yumie was born when Michitoshi found three very good alternatives of developing his research directions. Anyway, he was a scholar and teacher. As matter of fact, Michitoshi's father, namely my grandfather Shigema Kono was a school teacher and his last position was a school master. Michitoshi was a professor and I was a professor, too.

Michitoshi was a very methodical person. He was also strict and square. Reading his diaries or letters later I found that Michitoshi loved Hideko very much. Their marriage was typically a traditional and arranged one by their respective parents.

I do not remember exactly when, but in late 1944 or early 1945, aware of the possibilities of Hiroshima being bombed, my father Michitoshi decided to send his wife, Hideko, and younger son and daughters to Hideko's parental home, to Hoonji in Ino-mura, Shimane-ken, which was rural-agricultural and far from any big cities. The persons evacuated were: Hideko, born in 1911, 34 years old that time, Shozo born in 1937, 8 years old that time, Mariko, born in 1941, 4 years old and Yumie, your mother born in 1944, still an infant. On the other side, staying in Hiroshima were Michitoshi, born in 1902, 42 years old, Tomoyo, my step-grandmother (Shigema's second wife), born in 1868, 77 years old, Shigemi, born in 1930, 14 years old and Hiromi, born in 1932, 12 years old.

I think my father's decision was a good and thoughtful one, envisaging that bombings of Hiroshima were imminent. Anyway, Hideko, Shozo, Mariko and Yumie survived as evacuees. Out of the four who stayed in Hiroshima at that time, three were dead as of 1950, directly or indirectly caused by the bomb blast. I was the only survivor in 1950 and am still now.

March 15, 2013 Tokyo, Japan

著者紹介

河野英子（こうの　ひでこ）
1911（明治44）年、島根県浜田市井野に生まれる。生家（椿家）
は曹洞宗三宗派の一つの禅寺、報恩寺。
実践女学校を卒業後、1929（昭和4）年に河野通利と結婚し、
広島市に移り住み、4男2女の母となる。四男の通影は1940
年に乳児で死亡。
1945（昭和20）年8月6日、アメリカ軍の広島への原子爆弾
投下により、夫と次男宏臣を亡くす。
戦後、広島で被爆しながら生き延びた長男稠果と、いっしょに
疎開していて助かった他の3人の子どもたち、祥三、眞里子、
優三枝の5人で、島根県松江市に移り住み、料理店を営む。
子どもたちの成長を見届け、1995（平成7）年に没す。
生涯を通じて短歌に親しみ、著書に第一歌集『路』(1967年)と『草
の実』(1989年)がある。

家族写真　左から河野英子、夫通
利、三男祥三、長男稠果、次男宏臣。
1939（昭和14）年6月15日撮影

120

Profile: Author

HIDEKO KONO was born Hideko Tsubaki in 1911 in Ino, Hamada City, Shimane Prefecture, Japan. She was born into the Soto Sect of the Buddhist Temple Hoonji, one of the three sects of Zen Buddhism.

After completing secondary school at Jissen Jogakko, she was married to Michitoshi Kono in 1929 and relocated to Hiroshima. She had six children: Shigemi, Hiromi, Shozo, Michikage,Mariko, and Yumie.

Her husband Michitoshi and son Hiromi were killed in the atomic bombing of Hiroshima on August 6, 1945. Her son Shigemi Kono survived. She and her other children Shozo, Mariko, and Yumie survived as evacuees. Her son Michikage had died earlier in 1940 as an infant.

After the war, she relocated to Matsue, Shimane Prefecture, and became a restaurant owner.

She died in 1995 after seeing her children grow up.

She wrote Tanka poetry throughout her life and is the author of two published books of poetry, *Michi* (1967) and *Kusa No Mi* (1989) .

Family photo(p.120) Left to right, Hideko Kono,
Michitoshi Kono(husband), 3 brothers; Shozo,
Shigemi, Hiromi in 1939

編訳者・翻訳者・寄稿者紹介

河野優三枝（こうの　ゆみえ）

カナダ、ブリティッシュ・コロンビア州ビクトリア在住の画家。主に鉛筆画、油絵、テンペラ画を制作する。

1944（昭和 19）年、広島市生まれ。河野英子の次女。

1963 年に東京の女子美術大学を卒業し、1973 年にカナダに移住。バンフ美術大学、ニューヨーク美術大学、スコットランド彫刻工房などでのほか、数多くのワークショップに参加。カナダ文化庁賞ほか多数受賞。個展、グループ展をカナダと日本で定期的に行い、作品を発表。作品は、www.yumiekono.com で閲覧できる。

アリエル・オサリバン　Ariel O'Sullivan

カナダ、ブリティッシュ・コロンビア州ビクトリア在住の俳優、パフォーマンス詩人、アーティスト、画廊企画者。

1944 年、カナダ、オンタリオ州トロントに生まれる。バンフ美術大学、ビクトリア美術大学の学位を取得。オンタリオ州、ブリティッシュ・コロンビア州ビクトリアで若者劇場、音声のワークショップを受け、ビクトリア美術大学でアニメ制作者のために演技の指導をする。河野優三枝との共演を含め、カナダ国内全域にわたる数多くの場所で自作詩のパフォーマンスを行う。

河野稠果（こうの　しげみ）

麗澤大学名誉教授。

1930（昭和5）年、広島市生まれ。河野英子の長男。1945年8月6日、広島市で被爆したが生き残る。

1953年に山口大学文理学部を卒業後、フルブライト奨学金を得て、アメリカのブラウン大学大学院社会学部に入学。1958年、同大学大学院の博士号を取得。その後、厚生省人口問題研究所、国連人口問題研究所などの研究機関に勤め、日本の出生率低下について研究する。

1993（平成5）年から2006年まで麗澤大学国際経済学部教授。著書に『人口学への招待——少子・高齢化はどこまで解明されたか』（中公新書　2007年）ほか多数。

愛子・デイ　Iyko Day

アメリカ、マサチューセッツ州にあるマウントホリヨーク大学のエリザベスC.スモールの英語教授。アジア系アメリカ文学と視覚文化を研究し教えている。

1974年、カナダ、ブリティッシュ・コロンビア州グランド・フォークスに生まれる。河野優三枝の娘。河野英子の孫。

著書に『外国人資産——アジア人差別と入植者の植民地資本主義の論議』（デューク大学出版局　2016年）、共編著書に全集『批判的人種、土着性、関係性』（テンプル大学出版局）がある。

Profile: Editor, Translator, and Contributor

YUMIE KONO   is an artist based in Victoria, B.C., Canada who specializes in pencil drawing and oil and tempera painting.

She was born in Hiroshima City, Japan in 1944. She is Hideko Kono's daughter.

She holds a Bachelor of Fine Arts from Joshi Bijutsu Daigaku Women's College of Fine Arts in Tokyo Japan in 1963, and immigrated into Canada in 1973, and then has attended advanced workshops at the Banff School of Fine Arts, the New York School of Visual Arts, the Scottish Sculpture Workshop, and others. She is the recipient of numerous awards from the Canada Council for the Arts. Kono's artwork has been featured in solo and group exhibitions in Canada and Japan. For more information, please visit www.yumiekono.com.

ARIEL O'SULLIVAN is an actress, performance poet, visual artist, and gallery curator based in Victoria, B.C., Canada.

She was born in Toronto, Ontario, Canada in 1944.

She holds a degree from the Banff School of Fine Arts and advanced diplomas from the Victoria College of Art. She has led youth theatre and voice workshops in Ontario and Victoria B.C., and has taught Acting for Animators at the Victoria College of Art. She has performed her poetry in numerous venues across Canada and has which include performance collaborations with Yumie Kono.

SHIGEMI KONO is a Professor emeritus at Reitaku University, Kashiwa City, Japan.

He was born in Hiroshima City in 1930 as the eldest son of Hideko Kono. He survived the atomic bombing in Hiroshima on August 6, 1945.

He received his bachelor's degree in sociology at Yamaguchi National University in 1953, and held fellowships at Brown University and The University of Chicago. He received his doctorate at Brown in 1958.

Before taking a University position in 1993, he worked at the Population Division of the United Nations and numerous research institutes focused on population decline in Japan.

He is the author of numerous books and articles, including his latest book *Invitation to Demography* (Chuokoron Shinsho, 2007).

IYKO DAY is Elizabeth C. Small Professor of English at Mount Holyoke College in Massachusettes, USA. Her research and teaching focus on Asian American literature and visual culture.

She was born in Grand Forks, B.C., Canada in 1974. She is Yumie Kono's daughter, and Hideko Kono's grandchild.

She is the author of *Alien Capital: Asian Racialization and the Logic of Settler Colonial Capitalism* (Duke University Press, 2016), and she coedits the book series *Critical Race, Indigeneity, and Relationality* for Temple University Press.

ちちも姑も夫も子も死ぬ秋風に吹かれてあはれ一期一会は

朱色に燃え立つ垣根めぐらしておごそかに立つ河野家の墓

血を吐きて死にし姑かも子を生まぬ白き乳房は清らかなりき

姑と呼ぶつながり持ちて住みし家は無惨に散れり皿茶碗など

おとろへし腕に抱きてつぶやきの如き童話をくり返す姑

漂へる浮草われも根を持たぬ明日を未来と言ひがたきかも

餘燼（よじん）のぼる広島が目に浮び来る骨片さがす吾なりしかな

原爆に死にし姑（はは）なり老いまさぬ肢態は尚も水々（なおみずみず）しくて

ひたむきに生きる外なしそそけ立つ髪を水もて濡らし出で行く

着るもののなき身軽さやひらひらと裾を焼きたるスカート一枚

〈二男宏臣に〉

めぐり来る八月六日一握の灰もて汝を葬りたるのみ

20

131

短刀に妖しき光ふくませて子等の額に当ててしこともあり

防火訓練必至になせし愚かさよ焼けただれたる広島に立ち

櫛一つ形見の如く持ち歩く女終りてきびしき門出

夜ひそと貼られしビラか駅の前に平和と交戦の文字だけ赤し

一葉の写真に飾る黒リボン夫よ子の手を引きてゆきませ

なにによる命か明日を生きつぐは「何とかなるさ」皆自暴自棄

（三）

人心の定まらぬ夜に娘持つ父達銃をかまへて眠る

明日こそは敵の侵入あるべしと若者たちの夜毎さわげる

朝ぎりに手足冷え来し子を抱く死も易々と許されずして

悲しみに実りし吾子を脊に負ひて受刑の如く歩み初めぬ

16

相寄りて生き残りたる悲しみを語り合ふ時救急車来る

梅干しを一つ入れたる握り飯押しいただきつ涙流れぬ

失へるものばかりにて幾日経む焼けちぢまりしスカートをはき

行けど尚ゆけど続ける焦土にて鉄筋のみがよろぼひて立つ

くるしみの表情持たず死にたりし兵等よ日本勝つと思ひて

雨も陽も焦土うるほす糧ならず人焼く匂ひ天地に満つ

仮駅の夜露にねむる被爆者に渡さるるものパンと梅干

死者の匂ひ風に乗り来て幾万の霊（たま）飛び迷ふひろしまの上

悪臭を放つ死鳥の眼のくぼみ蛆（うじ）這ひ上がりあがりては落つ

かさこそと夫のつぶやき聞く如く骨壺をわがふりて悲しむ

仮駅に夫の骨持つどの汽車も女子供を取り残し行く

身辺の人ことごとく逝かしめて吾が呆然とありし幾日

おびただしく牛馬斃れし川砂を満潮なれば浸しゆくなり

双乳もあらはに見せて妻狂乱炎天あかき血を流す河

骨壺を抱きて居ればうつせみの夫とわれなり赤き花園

民族の亡び嘆けるうから等と配給パンをむさぼり食べる

次々と人は恐怖の中に死ぬ世界の滅び近づくを見つ

板の上に白く盛りたる骨片は涙枯れたる人が持ち去る

（二）

幾千の命吸ひたる川の面に魚透きて見ゆまこと平和に

地をゆりて魂（たま）泣く声はどよもせりあまねく降れる月光の中

142   9

頬焼けて娘死にたりみずからを絶ちしあはれも数多ければ

嫁ぎゆく夢にふくらむ黒髪をじりじりと焼く地獄のさまか

肌寒く目覚めし夜半に聞く死者の怨嗟の声は地をどよもせり

悲しみは越へてきびしき顔となるおのもおのもに骨ひろひつつ

又一人死にたるらしき収容所の裏をひっそり車の音す

一文の銭も持たねばぼろぼろの影ひき乍ら受けし一椀

累々と死体重なるその前にむしろ敷きつめ誰も眠りぬ

悲しみは言葉とならず只深きねむりを欲りて死者と並びぬ

6

145

寸秒をおかず次々斃（たお）れゆく兵等の顔を被（おお）うものなし

広島に生物（いきもの）絶ゆと言ひつぎて忽（たちま）ちさわぐ群衆心理

よたよたと醜き人の顔ばかり夕べの風に吹かれゆくなり

民族の滅び見せたり中空（なかぞら）に星が小さきまばたきを見す

崩れ去るどよめきの中生れねば死なざるものを火の粉飛び飛ぶ

血縁を求め疲るる人の群汗にまみれし我もその一人

4

無気味とも青き炎に光りつつ骨さらばへて蠅（はえ）につつかる

怒りにも疲れし吾等一盛りの骨頂きて帰り来りぬ

ひるも夜（よ）もくすぶり燃えつ須臾（しゅゆ）にして命うばひし何を憎まむ

（一）

広島の夜の色彩に放つりん青々と人のたましひが燃ゆ

焼跡も真夏の雨は降りそそぐ濡れ光れるは誰の骨ぞも

原爆の歌

河野英子歌集

原爆の歌　河野英子歌集
2023 年 4 月 20 日　第 1 刷発行

著　　者──河野英子
編　　訳──河野優三枝
英　　訳──アリエル・オサリバン
装　　幀──渡辺美知子
編　　集──関宏子
発行者──遠藤真広
発行所──木犀社
〒 390-0303　長野県松本市浅間温泉 2-1-20
TEL（0263）88-6852　FAX（0263）88-6862
http://www.mksei.com
印刷所──信毎書籍印刷
製本所──渋谷文泉閣

ISBN 978-4-89618-071-8 C0092